# The Story of Chester the Chow-Chow

Terri L Hall and Denise L Babeaux

PUBLISH AMERICA

PublishAmerica
Baltimore

First printing

ISBN: 978-1-4560-3748-2
PUBLISHED BY PUBLISHAMERICA, LLLP
www.publishamerica.com
Baltimore

Printed in the United States of America

On a cool February morning in a small town in the dessert of Southern California, a litter of Chow Chow Puppies were born. These little puppies were so small and were just like little balls of fur. There were black ones and red ones; they were so small and precious. They snuggled close to their mother for warmth and protection.

In this litter of puppies, there were 3 little boy puppies and two little girl puppies. The puppies would stay with their mother until they were old enough to go to a new home, where they would be loved and cared for.

The home they were born at was a nice safe place for now, but Chow Chow puppies grow to be 60 or 70 lbs. Once the puppies were weaned, each puppy would need to have a good home to call their own. It is important to remember when choosing a pet to select a pet that suits your family. Your pet will be with you for years to come.

The puppies grew each week, and they learned something new each day. Once they opened their eyes, they could see their mother, but they knew her by her smell already. The children of the family loved the little puppies. After three weeks, the puppies were up walking around the house. Once they made their way around the corner of the hall and into the living room, those puppies were all over the house. This was a fun time for the little puppies and the children.

The puppies were now 6 weeks old and it was time for the children to let them find a new home. The parents explained that the puppies would grow, and they needed to find new homes, where they can grow and have their own families. The family placed an ad in the paper.

"Cute and Adorable Chow Chow puppies, six weeks old, for sale to good homes."

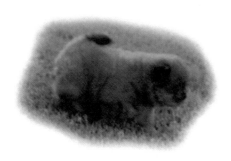

Well what do you know... sure enough, there was a family just a few miles away that was looking for a Chow Chow puppy and they saw the ad in the paper. The family called the number in the paper and went right over to see the puppies. When the family arrived, they saw the little puppies running all over the house- how darling they were. They picked up each puppy and held it- how soft and adorable they were. The family could only pick one, and it was such a hard choice. Finally, the family settled on the red little boy puppy.

The family children picked up the puppy, and they were ready to take him home. The children were very excited and knew they had selected a great addition to the family. Now the older sister, Terri, asked her younger sister, Denise, if she wanted to hold the little puppy, and of course, Denise said, "Yes." Well no longer than two seconds passed, Terri told her, "Okay, that is enough give him back." The girls were going to love this little puppy.

When the girls got the puppy home, they knew he was hot. He had a lot of hair, so they placed him in front of the fan, and that is where he loved to lay for his nap.

The fan blew cool air all over the puppy, and he slept there with his toys. The little puppy was also about to meet some new friends.

Now the girls had the puppy for a whole day, and they knew he needed a name. Right now, he was a brownish-reddish color, but he would grow to be a red Chow Chow. The girls thought hard to find a name for the puppy.

"Harry?"

"NO."

"Fred?"

"NO."

"Sam?"

"NO!"

Then they said "Chester."

"Yes, Chester, that fits the little puppy perfectly."

So it was, the little puppy would be named Chester.

Now it was time for Chester to meet his new friends. He was having a very busy day. His new friends were three cats and they were named Scarlet, Taz, and General Lee. They would be great friends for Chester.

Chester made friends with the cats, and they played together all through the house. Scarlet was the mother cat of Taz and General Lee, and they were glad to have a new member to the family. They all lived together happily.

Well, Chester was growing bigger already, and Chester needed a place outside to call his own. So, Terri and Denise decided a big doghouse would suit Chester just fine. Terri and Denise ask their father to build Chester a dog house and they promised to help.

Now, Chester was excited about his home outside. He loved to run around the yard, and he was anxious to get his house. Once the dog house was finished, it looked just like a big red barn. Chester loved his dog house, but he still spent most HOT days and nights in the cool house by his fan

One day, a few months later, the father came home from work. He explained to the family that they would be moving. He explained the move was a long move, and showed Terri and Denise that the move was all the way across the United States. The family was moving from California to Georgia, and it was a long trip from what Terri and Denise could tell. Chester had grown to be pretty big dog by now, and he loved to ride with the family.

As the days passed, the family began to pack their belongings, and prepare for the long trip to a new state and a new home. The girls would miss their friends, but knew the move was important for their family. The girls made sure Chester was ready too. They packed all his toys in a special basket just for him. As Chester grew, the girls noticed Chester's tongue was black. Their father explained that the black tongue it is part of the Chow Chow breed. The girls were glad Chester was not sick.

Chester did not understand why they were moving, but he loved to ride, and he was excited he was going to travel. Once everything was packed, it was all aboard. Chester took a seat by the window, so he could see out.

Now, Chester kept that spot in the car the whole trip, and he saw a lot of interesting animals out of that window. Chester just sat and starred out of that window paying close attention to everything.

On this trip, the family would travel through many states to get to their new home. Chester kept a close eye out the window. Chester saw date palms when leaving California.

Chester and the family saw buffalo and rabbits out in the fields along the trip. It was fun to see the animals.

There were a lot of pasture cows along the way, and the father explained about the different breeds.

Finally, after four days of traveling, the family reached their new home. Chester loved his new backyard, and he just sat down to look around. Chester had plenty of room to roam around.

Chester went all around the backyard checking out all the plants, flowers, and the pool. Chester loved the family's new home.

Now, it was hot in the summer, so the family decided
Chester needed a new haircut. Chester got a lion cut,
and he was cool and happy.

The family enjoyed swimming, and every time before swimming, they would check the skimmer. Chester checked the skimmer too. Just as soon as the lid was off, Chester would place his head right in the skimmer.

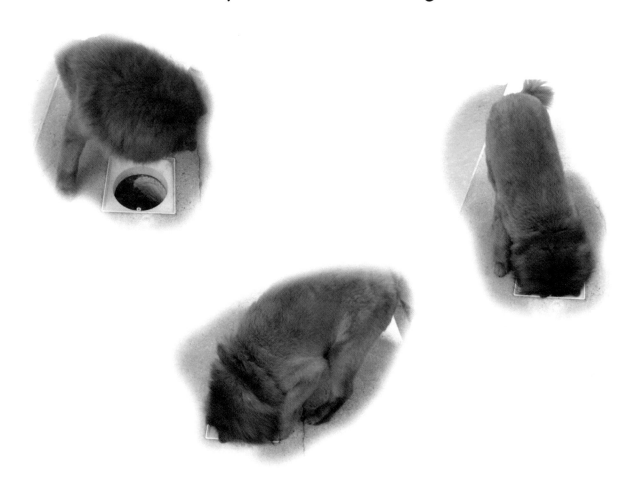

Chester wanted to make sure there were no lizards in the pool before the kids got in to swim.

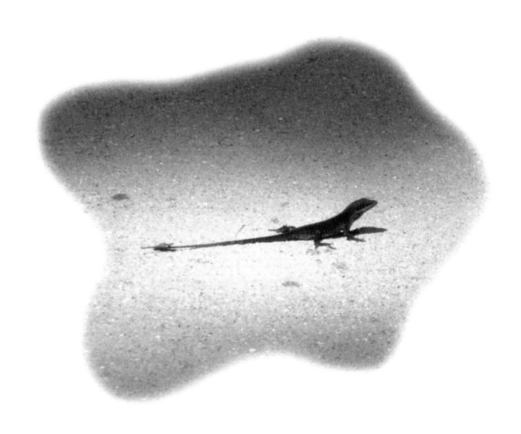

Chester enjoyed all the beautiful flowers in the backyard, and loved to chase the shadows of the butterflies. It was fun to watch Chester follow the shadows.

After about two years, the family decided to return to California and Chester would, once again, travel the distance. The family was excited to return to California, and the trip that they would make to return. Once again, the items were packed, the trip was planned, and the family set off to travel through the mountains.

The family enjoyed the fun time traveling along the mountain roads.

Chester saw Squirrels and lots of ducks on the trip back to California.

There were woodcarvers all along the mountain villages.

And there were horses too.

The family saw sheep and feed yard cattle. Chester was very curious about the steers at the feed yard.

Once the family arrived back to California, Chester had to explore his new surroundings.

Chester went to the backyard and back to the frontyard- so much room to roam he had.

Early one morning, Chester was awoken to the sound of parrots- wild parrots. Chester had to go see what all the noise was about. There were a lot of parrots, green ones just sitting in the trees and on the telephone poles.

Chester could not take his eyes off all those parrots.

Now, Chester could see all the parrots out on the line, then all of a sudden, two of them flew off. The line swayed down, and one parrot turned upside down- he almost fell off. The parrots now visit, every morning.

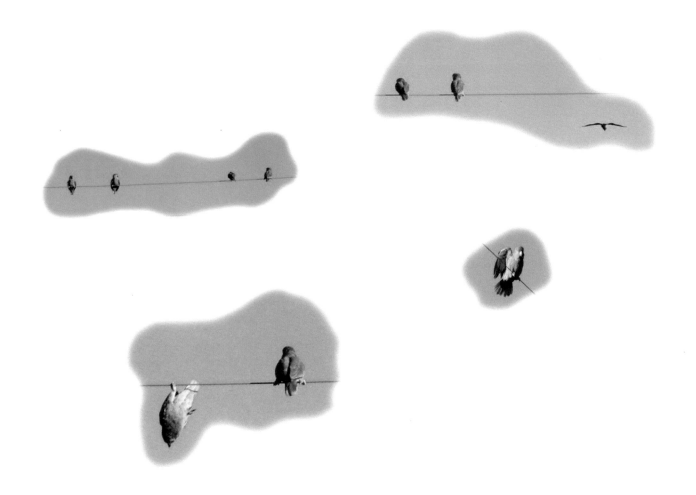

Chester loves his new home and he loves to go to Dog Beach, where he can run and play. It helps keep Chester healthy and friendly!

The dogs run and play at Dog Beach!

Chester keeps his lion cut in the summer months; it helps keep him cool. He visits the Doggie Lodge on a regular basis for proper care of his coat. A clean coat helps keep Chester happy and healthy.

Remember, when deciding on your family pet, consider what type of pet will best fit your family. Always be kind to your pet, and in return, they will give you many years of happiness and joy!

The End

# Would you like to see your manuscript become a book?

If you are interested in becoming a PublishAmerica author, please submit your manuscript for possible publication to us at:

**acquisitions@publishamerica.com**

You may also mail in your manuscript to:

**PublishAmerica
PO Box 151
Frederick, MD 21705**

# www.publishamerica.com

CPSIA information can be obtained
at www.ICGtesting.com
Printed in the USA
LVIC041434070113

314706LV00003B